A.D.D. not B.A.D.

Written by Audrey Penn and illustrated by Monica Dunsky Wyrick

CLARK PUBLIC LIBRARY
303 WESTFIELD AVENUE
CLARK, NJ 07066
732-388-5999

D1604618

Tanglewood Press

Terre Haute, IN

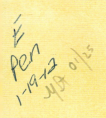

To my very own Jayme Jumpingbean.
- AP

To my own dynamite dudes, and to
Ms. Green's class at Olive Chapel in Apex.
- MW

Published by Tanglewood Press, Inc., 2006.
First published by the Child Welfare League of America, 2003.

© 2003 by Audrey Penn. All rights reserved. Neither this book nor any part may be reproduced or transmitted in any form or by any means, electronic or mechanical, including photocopying, microfilming, and recording, or by any information storage and retrieval system, without permission in writing from the publisher.

Tanglewood Press: P. O. Box 3009, Terre Haute, IN 47803, www.tanglewoodbooks.com

10 9 8 7 6 5 4 3 2 1

Text design by Michael Rae

Printed in China

ISBN 0-9749303-7-7
    978-0-9749303-7-4

Library of Congress Cataloging-in-Publication Data

Penn, Audrey, 1947-
  A.D.D. not B.A.D. / written by Audrey Penn and illustrated by Monica
Dunsky Wyrick.
    p. cm.
  Summary: Jimmy Jumpingbean and his teacher, Mr. Jugardor, demonstrate to the class why Jimmy's attention deficit disorder makes it hard for him to sit still.
  ISBN 0-9749303-7-7 (alk. paper)
  [1. Attention-deficit hyperactivity disorder--Fiction. 2. Schools--Fiction.] I. Wyrick, Monica, ill. II. Title.
  PZ7.P38448Ad 2006
  [E]--dc22
                                           2006003729

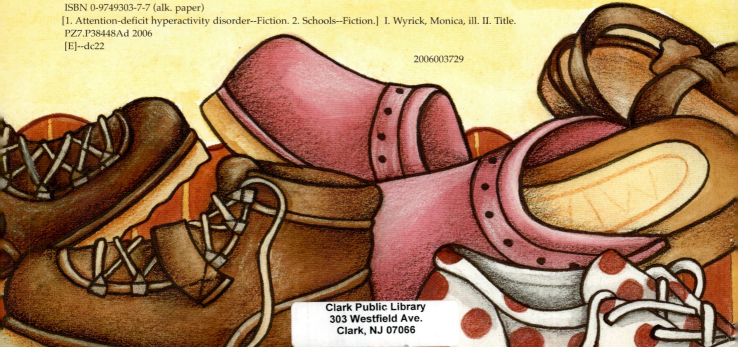

Clark Public Library
303 Westfield Ave.
Clark, NJ 07066

Foreword

by Paul George Prunier, M.D.

As a practicing child-adolescent-adult psychiatrist, I frequently diagnose and treat Attention Deficit Hyperactivity Disorder (ADHD). I recognize that some controversy exists as to why this condition has "suddenly" become so common. On the other hand, I have come to know that children, teenagers, and adults truly suffer from ADHD. Because the problem behaviors so common to this condition are easily confused with "bad" behavior, children with ADHD often find themselves socially isolated or scapegoated. Yet for those who suffer from this condition, such behaviors are in no way intentional.

Any effort to help other children (and their parents) understand the dynamics of this condition is both important and laudable, and I therefore welcome the addition of *A.D.D. not B.A.D.* to a growing body of such works. Children who do not have ADHD need to understand that the ways in which they react to their peers who have ADHD and other medical conditions can impact the overall outcome of those individuals. As our society struggles to embrace various groups of people, children who have ADHD must be included and assisted, so that they might also have an opportunity to share in the American dream.

75%

3 ¾

348 =

Mr. Jugardor's students were very excited. "We're going to have some fun," he told everyone. "The first thing I want you to do is to take off your shoes and line them up in the front of the room."

At first, Mr. Jugardor's students giggled. No one would take off their shoes until somebody else did first.

"Sally Brave is doing it," said
Freddie Follow. "So I will, too."

Soon, all of Mr. Jugardor's students took off their shoes and lined them up in the front of the room.

"Now," said Mr. Jugardor, "I want you to pick out a pair of shoes that you know won't fit, carefully step inside them, and walk around the classroom."

Mr. Jugardor's students twittered and giggled the whole time they tried on each other's shoes. When Willow Walkright tried on Brucie Big's tennis shoes, she stumbled over the extra-long toes. When Betty Widebow tried on Tiny Highstep's sandals, her heels stuck out. Some students tripped and bumped into each other. Some students flipped and flopped in shoes that felt as big as next year's holiday slippers.

Mr. Jugardor watched and laughed. "That was a very silly thing to do, wasn't it?" he asked his class. "But it can be very helpful to understand what it's like to walk in someone else's shoes. Sometimes it can be very comfortable. And sometimes, it can be very uncomfortable. It's hard to know how other people feel, or what it's like to be someone else," explained Mr. Jugardor. "So it's very important that we try and put ourselves in their place. Sort of like wearing their shoes. Do you think you can remember that?"

When his class yelled, "Yes!" Mr. Jugardor said, "Good! You may now have your own shoes back."

Jimmy Jumpingbean jumped back into his own shoes and hopped back to his desk in the very last row of the classroom. He had enjoyed playing the game very much. He grinned and giggled as he rocked in his chair, and swung his legs, and rapped on his desk with his pencil.

"Shh!" said Sandy Sitstill.
"Stop tapping!" shouted Brittany Calm.
"I can't hear Mr. Jugardor."

Mr. Jugardor had another surprise. He called his students over to the bookcase under the row of windows.

"Hi, Jimmy Jumpingbean," said Mr. Jugardor.

"Hi, Mr. Jugardor," laughed Jimmy Jumpingbean.

Everybody giggled, even Jimmy Jumpingbean.

"Jimmy," said Mr. Jugardor, with a wink of his right eye. "I want you to show your friends what it's like when you have to sit still in class, or at an assembly, or in a movie that you really want to see."

Jimmy sat down in a chair and placed his folded hands on his lap. He grinned at Mr. Jugardor and waited quietly for almost one full minute. Suddenly, Jimmy's legs began to swing, and his chair began to rock. He started bouncing up and down as if he were going to pop!

"Thank you, Jimmy," said Mr. Jugardor. "You may stand up now. You did a very good job."

"I don't think he did a very good job at all," said Simon Showoff. "I can sit in a chair for hours. Jimmy's always jumping around the room."

"That's right," said Mr. Jugardor. "And I'm going to show you why very soon. Jimmy has something called Attention Deficit Disorder, or A.D.D."

"And," added Jimmy, "hyperactivity."

To explain A.D.D. and hyperactivity, Mr. Jugardor uncovered a box full of ladybugs and showed them to his students. Some of his students said, "Ah!" Some of his students went, "Ooh!" And some of his students said, "Ech!"

Mr. Jugardor laughed. "I just love ladybugs," he told everyone. "They're pretty and helpful, and they never bite or sting. Now," he asked. "Who is the bravest person in class?"

Everyone raised their hand.

"Good," said Mr. Jugardor. "I want everyone to go back to your seat and sit very quietly. Everyone except for Jimmy Jumpingbean. He will be helping me."

It was very hard for the students in Mr. Jugardor's class to sit still and be quiet because of all the excitement. But everyone did just fine.

Mr. Jugardor and Jimmy Jumpingbean took the box full of ladybugs and walked around the room. Everyone got to hold one, except for Jimmy Jumpingbean.

"Now," said Mr. Jugardor, as he and Jimmy Jumpingbean walked to the front of the classroom. "When I say go, I want each of you to put your ladybug down the back of your shirt, then sit very, very still." When the students laughed and shouted, "Oh, no!" Mr. Jugardor called out...

Some of the students squealed with delight when they put the ladybugs down their shirts.

Some of the students screamed with laughter when they put the ladybugs down their shirts.

And some of the students yelled, "Ooh, yuck!" when they put the ladybugs down their shirts.

Mr. Jugardor and Jimmy Jumpingbean giggled, too, as the kids in class sat in their
seats, hands folded neatly, waiting quietly.
They made it for almost ten whole seconds.

Suddenly, Sandy Sitstill jumped to her feet and flapped her arms like a butterfly. Brittany Calm leaped out of her chair and ran circles around her desk. And Simon Showoff slipped off his seat and onto the floor where he wriggled like a worm in a rainstorm.

Principal Patience came into Mr. Jugardor's classroom and saw twenty-four students hopping and jumping, squeaking and running. The only quiet student in the entire classroom was Jimmy Jumpingbean.

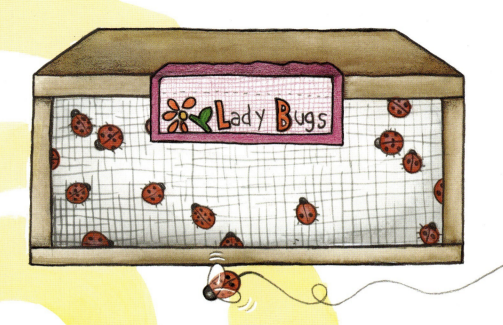

Mr. Jugardor and Jimmy Jumpingbean collected all of the ladybugs and returned them to their covered box.

"Sometimes," Jimmy Jumpingbean told his classmates, "I feel like I have a whole box full of ladybugs down my shirt. But if I rock, or sway, or swing my legs, it makes the bugginess go away."

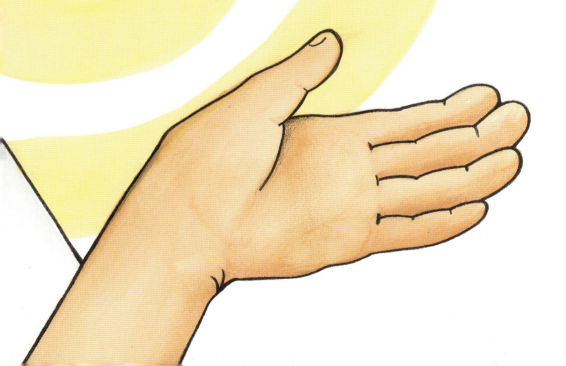

Do you know what Mr. Jugardor's students
said about that? They said, "Oh! Okay!

"He's not **B ★ A ★ D**. He's not **BAD** at all.
He's not **B ★ A ★ D**. He's not rude.
He's **A ★ D ★ D**. Jimmy's **A ★ D ★ D**—
       He's an...